WELCOME TO
PASSPORT TO READING
A beginning reader's ticket to a brand-new world!

Every book in this program is designed to build read-along and read-alone skills, level by level, through engaging and enriching stories. As the reader turns each page, he or she will become more confident with new vocabulary, sight words, and comprehension.

These PASSPORT TO READING levels will help you choose the perfect book for every reader.

READING TOGETHER
Read short words in simple sentence structures together to begin a reader's journey.

READING OUT LOUD
Encourage developing readers to sound out words in more complex stories with simple vocabulary.

READING INDEPENDENTLY
Newly independent readers gain confidence reading more complex sentences with higher word counts.

READY TO READ MORE
Readers prepare for chapter books with fewer illustrations and longer paragraphs.

This book features sight words from the educator-supported Dolch Sight Words List. This encourages the reader to recognize commonly used vocabulary words, increasing reading speed and fluency.

For more information, please visit passporttoreadingbooks.com.

Enjoy the journey!

Little, Brown and Company

Hachette Book Group
1290 Avenue of the Americas, New York, NY 10104
Visit us at lb-kids.com

Little, Brown and Company is a division of Hachette Book Group, Inc.
The Little, Brown name and logo are trademarks of Hachette Book Group, Inc.
The publisher is not responsible for websites (or their content) that are not owned by the publisher.

First Edition: April 2017

ISBNs: 978-0-316-36187-3 (pbk.), 978-0-316-36189-7 (ebook),
978-0-316-55377-3 (ebook), 978-0-316-55376-6 (ebook)

Library of Congress Control Number: 2016947538

10 9 8 7 6 5 4 3 2 1

CW

Printed in the United States of America

Passport to Reading titles are leveled by independent reviewers applying the standards developed
by Irene Fountas and Gay Su Pinnell in *Matching Books to Readers: Using Leveled Books in
Guided Reading*, Heinemann, 1999.

Licensed By:

Photo credits: page 3 photo of underwater scene © Christopher Gardiner; page 6 photo of coral reef © Discovod; page 7 photo of killer whale © Christian Musat; page 7 photo of sea lion © kroko; page 7 photo of octopus © Andrea Izzotti; page 7 photo of jumping dolphins © Tory Kallman; page 8 photo of group of sharks © VisionDive; page 8 photo of great white shark © Sergey Uryadnikov; page 9 photo of shark pup © Rich Carey; page 10 photo of gills © Svetlana Aramileva; page 10 and 11 photo of shark © Yann Hubert; page 12 and 13 photo of great white shark © Martin Prochazkacz; page 13 photo of school bus © Nerthuz; page 13 photo of reef shark © VisionDive; page 14 of wobbegong © martin_hristov; page 14 photo of hammerhead shark © Martin Prochazkacz; page 14 and 15 photo of whale shark © kaschibo; page 15 photo of tiger shark © Greg Amptman; page 15 photo of basking shark © Corbis/VCG; page 16 photo of blue whale © Ethan Daniels; page 16 and 17 photo of humpback whale © Gudkov Andrey; page 17 photo of krill © Dmytro Pylypenko; page 18 photo of dolphin pod © Willyam Bradberry; page 19 photo of dolphin © Mike Price; page 20 of seal © critterbiz; page 20 and 21 photo of otter © worldswildlifewonders; page 21 photo of sea snake © Rich Carey; page 21 photo of sea turtle © Isabelle Kuehn; page 22 photo of octopus © Olga Visavi; page 22 of squid © Amanda Nicholls; page 23 photo of starfish © Laura Dinraths; page 23 photo of jellyfish © H.Tanaka; page 23 photo of cuttlefish © bikeriderlondon; page 24 photo of sawfish © Jill Lang; page 24 photo of clown fish © orlandin; page 24 and 25 photo of ray © stephan kerkhofs; page 25 of flying fish © feathercollector; page 25 of puffer fish © Beth Swanson; page 27 photo of boat © Geri Lavrov; page 27 photo of cleaning crew © Luis Díaz Devesa; page 28 photo of rehabilitation duck © Justin Sullivan; page 29 photo of rehabilitation seal © JLRphotography; page 32 photo of tiger shark © Greg Amptman; page 32 photo of sea turtle © Isabelle Kuehn; page 32 photo of octopus © Olga Visavi; page 32 photo of starfish © Laura Dinraths.

SHARKS
& OTHER SEA LIFE!

by Trey King

L B

LITTLE, BROWN AND COMPANY
New York   Boston

"I am making a manual for
new Rescue Bots," Cody says.
"Can you help me learn about sharks?"

"Of course," says High Tide.
"But only if I can teach you about
other sea life as well."

Let us go underwater.
Good thing I can change into a submarine.

killer whale

sea lion

octopus

dolphin

There are over 230 thousand species
of marine life.
Marine is word for things
living in the sea.

Sharks are a type of fish.

They are known as dangerous creatures.

But they do not attack humans

as often as many people think.

Baby sharks are called **pups**. When they are born, they know how to take care of themselves. They can already swim.

shark pup

Servo heard someone say pup!

Sharks never stop swimming.
Swimming is how they breathe.
As they move forward, water passes
through their **gills** and turns into
air inside their bodies.

gills

Sharks do not have a single
bone in their body.
Their skeleton is made up of
cartilage—just like human
ears and noses.

What wonderful
creatures! Though
not as cool as my
shark sub.

Great white sharks are found mostly in cool water close to the coast. Each one has 300 sharp teeth!

Sharks lose their teeth all the time—but their teeth grow back quickly! Most sharks have five rows of teeth or more.

That's a lot of teeth! A human only has 32 teeth.

FUN FACT

Most great white sharks are about 15 feet long. But some have been as long as 20 feet—that's half the length of a bus!

13

There are around 440
different kinds of sharks.
The smallest is a dwarf lantern shark,
which is smaller than a human hand.
The largest is the whale shark, which
is also the largest living species of fish.

hammerhead shark

wobbegong

whale shark

tiger shark

basking shark

15

blue whale

Whales are different from sharks.
Like humans, whales are warm-blooded.
They need air to live, but they can hold
their breaths for a long time.

The blue whale is the largest
mammal in the world.
They feed on tiny, shrimplike
creatures called krill.

krill

humpback whale

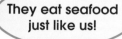

Don't forget about dolphins!

Dolphins are also mammals that live in water. They squeak and whistle to talk to one another.

They are very friendly and playful. Scientists believe they are one of the smartest animals on Earth.

bottlenose dolphin

The ocean is filled with many
kinds of animals.
Some are **mammals**—
like seals and otters.

seal

otter

Others are **reptiles**—
like sea snakes and turtles.

reef snake

sea turtle

Sea turtles are one of the planet's oldest creatures.

21

octopus

Octopuses and **squids** are a different type of ocean creature.

They have eight arms and are related to snails— but they do not have a hard outer shell.

squid

There are 28 thousand different types of fish. They come in all kinds of shapes and sizes.

sawfish

clown fish

flying fish

puffer fish

spotted eagle ray

FUN FACT

Rays are fish, too. They are closely related to sharks, but they have very flat bodies.

Sometimes accidents happen.

Today, oil has spilled into the ocean.

Luckily, everyone is prepared to help.

People work together.

They use trucks and boats to help

the injured animals.

First, rescuers help the animals
get better after the accident.
This is called **rehabilitation**.

Once the animals are cleaned up
and healthy again, they are released
back into the wild.

"I learned a lot today," Cody says. "I cannot wait to share it with others. I wonder what my next training manual topic should be...."

31

Hello, Rescue Team cadets!
Go back and read this story again—
but this time, see if you can find these words!

tiger shark

sea turtle

octopus

starfish